Dear Parents:

Congratulations! Your child is taking the first steps on an exciting journey. The destination? Independent reading!

STEP INTO READING® will help your child get there. The program offers five steps to reading success. Each step includes fun stories and colorful art or photographs. In addition to original fiction and books with favorite characters, there are Step into Reading Non-Fiction Readers, Phonics Readers and Boxed Sets, Sticker Readers, and Comic Readers—a complete literacy program with something to interest every child.

Learning to Read, Step by Step!

Ready to Read   Preschool–Kindergarten
• big type and easy words • rhyme and rhythm • picture clues
For children who know the alphabet and are eager to begin reading.

Reading with Help   Preschool–Grade 1
• basic vocabulary • short sentences • simple stories
For children who recognize familiar words and sound out new words with help.

Reading on Your Own   Grades 1–3
• engaging characters • easy-to-follow plots • popular topics
For children who are ready to read on their own.

Reading Paragraphs   Grades 2–3
• challenging vocabulary • short paragraphs • exciting stories
For newly independent readers who read simple sentences with confidence.

Ready for Chapters   Grades 2–4
• chapters • longer paragraphs • full-color art
For children who want to take the plunge into chapter books but still like colorful pictures.

STEP INTO READING® is designed to give every child a successful reading experience. The grade levels are only guides; children will progress through the steps at their own speed, developing confidence in their reading.

Remember, a lifetime love of reading starts with a single step!

Visit us on the Web!
StepIntoReading.com
rhcbooks.com

Educators and librarians, for a variety of teaching tools, visit us at
RHTeachersLibrarians.com

ISBN 978-0-593-30421-1 (trade) — ISBN 978-0-593-30422-8 (lib. bdg.)

Printed in the United States of America

10 9 8 7 6 5 4 3 2 1

nickelodeon

Butterbean's café

Soccer Star!

by Tex Huntley

illustrated by MJ Illustrations

Random House 🏠 New York

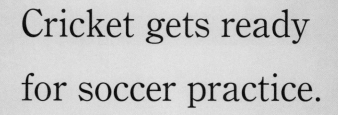

Cricket gets ready
for soccer practice.

Today the coach
will choose
a team captain.

Butterbean, Dazzle,
and Poppy make
a chocolate treat
for soccer practice.

Uh-oh!

Cricket should not
play soccer
in the café.

Cricket plays outside.

The soccer ball bounces
back into the kitchen!

Oh, no!
The ball broke
the chocolate
soccer treat!

The soccer ball bounces
back into the kitchen!

Oh, no!
The ball broke
the chocolate
soccer treat!

Cricket tries to fix it.

The pieces are

very loose.

Later at practice,
Spork and Spatch play
near the treat.

Their ball hits
the table it is on.
The treat
falls apart again!

Spork and Spatch
cannot play soccer
because they broke
the treat.

The coach says
Cricket is captain.

Cricket feels bad.
Will she still be
captain if she says
what she did?

Cricket has to tell
the truth.
She broke the treat.

Spatch and Spork
can play again!

Cricket is still
captain . . . because
she told the truth!

Butterbean's magic
Soccer Bean
saves the day.

The treat turns into yummy little soccer ball sweets!

Hooray for
the soccer team!